A Note to Parents

Read to your child...

★ Reading aloud is one of the best ways to develop your child's love of reading. Read together at least 20 minutes each day.

★ Laughter is contagious! Read with feeling. Show your child that reading is fun.

★ Take time to answer questions your child may have about the story. Linger over pages that interest your child.

...and your child will read to you.

★ Follow cues from your child to know when he wants to join in the reading.

★ Support your young reader. Give him a word whenever he asks for it.

★ Praise your child as he progresses. Your encouraging words will build his confidence.

You can help your Level 1 reader.

★ Reading begins with knowing how a book works. Show your child the title and where the story begins.

★ Ask your child to find picture clues on each page. Talk about what is happening in the story.

★ Point to the words as you read so your child can make the connection between the print and the story.

★ Ask your child to point to words she knows.

★ Let your child supply the rhyming words.

Most of all, enjoy your reading time together!

—Bernice Cullinan, Ph.D.,
Professor of Reading, New York University

Published by Reader's Digest Children's Books
Reader's Digest Road, Pleasantville, NY U.S.A. 10570-7000 and
Reader's Digest Children's Publishing Limited,
The Ice House, 124-126 Walcot Street, Bath UK BA1 5BG
Copyright © 1999 Reader's Digest Children's Publishing, Inc.
All rights reserved. Reader's Digest Children's Books is a trademark and
Reader's Digest and All-Star Readers are registered trademarks of
The Reader's Digest Association, Inc. Fisher-Price trademarks are used
under license from Fisher-Price, Inc., a subsidiary of
Mattel, Inc., East Aurora, NY 14052 U.S.A.
©2000 Mattel, Inc. All Rights Reserved.
Printed in Hong Kong.
10 9 8 7

Library of Congress Cataloging-in-Publication Data

Kueffner, Sue.
    Our new baby / by Sue Kueffner ; illustrated by Dorothy Stott.
        p.   cm. — (All-star readers. Level 1)
    Summary: A sister initially resents but then comes to love her new baby brother.
    ISBN 1-57584-292-0 (pbk. : alk. paper)
    [1. Babies—Fiction. 2. Brothers and sisters—Fiction. 3. Stories in rhyme.]
I. Stott, Dorothy M., ill. II. Title. III. Series.
PZ8.3.H7577Ou   1999   [E]—dc21   98-49564

Our New Baby

by Sue Kueffner

illustrated by Dorothy Stott

All-Star Readers®

Reader's Digest Children's Books™

Pleasantville, New York • Montréal, Québec

We have a new baby.

He is a pest.

We have a new baby.

Mom likes him the best.

What makes him so great?

He can not even talk.

Just look at me skate!

He can not even walk.

Boy, does he yell!

He likes to eat mush.

Boy, does he smell!

We all have to hush.

It is not bad

when he is asleep.

I kiss him like Dad.

He smiles in his sleep.

I have a new baby.

He is no pest!

He is MY baby.

He likes me the best.

Color in the star next to each word you can read.

☆ a	☆ his	☆ not
☆ all	☆ hush	☆ our
☆ asleep	☆ I	☆ pest
☆ at	☆ in	☆ skate
☆ baby	☆ is	☆ sleep
☆ bad	☆ it	☆ smell
☆ best	☆ just	☆ smiles
☆ boy	☆ kiss	☆ so
☆ can	☆ like	☆ talk
☆ dad	☆ look	☆ the
☆ does	☆ makes	☆ to
☆ eat	☆ me	☆ walk
☆ even	☆ mom	☆ we
☆ great	☆ mush	☆ what
☆ have	☆ my	☆ when
☆ he	☆ new	☆ yell
☆ him	☆ no	